...AE AN CHLÁIR
CLARE COUNTY LIBRARY
Library
WITHDRAWN FROM STOCK

D0586165

Leabharlann Chontae an Chláir

CL208771

The Cats in
Krasinski Square

The Cats in Krasinski Square

Karen Hesse

Illustrated by Wendy Watson

CLARE COUNTY LIBRARIES

F

FRANCES LINCOLN
CHILDREN'S BOOKS

Text copyright © Karen Hesse 2004
Illustrations copyright © Wendy Watson 2004

First published in the USA by Scholastic Press
Published in Great Britain in 2007 by
Frances Lincoln Children's Books, 4 Torriano Mews,
Torriano Avenue, London NW5 2RZ
www.franceslincoln.com

All rights reserved

No part of this publication may be reproduced, stored in a retrieval system, or transmitted,
in any form, or by any means, electrical, mechanical, photocopying, recording or otherwise
without the prior written permission of the publisher or a licence permitting restricted copying.
In the United Kingdom such licences are issued by the Copyright Licensing Agency,
Saffron House, 6-10 Kirby Street, London EC1N 8TS.

British Library Cataloguing in Publication Data is available on request.

ISBN 978-1-84507-701-3

Illustrated with pencil, ink and watercolours

Text type is set in Antykwa Poltawskiego, designed and cast by a Polish typographer,
Adam Jerzy Poltawski, in the late 1940s. The display type is set in Dalliance Roman.

Book design by Elizabeth B. Parisi

Printed in China
1 3 5 7 9 8 6 4 2

The cats
come
from the cracks in the Wall,
the dark corners,
the openings in the rubble.

CLARE COUNTY LIBRARIES

They know

I can offer only

a gentle hand,

a tender voice.

They have no choice but to come.

They belonged once to someone.

They slept on sofa cushions

and ate from crystal dishes.

They purred,

furrowing the chests,

nuzzling the chins of their beloveds.

Now they have no one to kiss their

velvet heads. I whisper,

"I have no food to spare."

The cats don't care.

I can keep my fistful of bread,

my watery soup, my potato,

so much more

than my friend Michal gets

behind the Wall of the Ghetto.

The cats don't need me feeding them.

They get by nicely on mice.

I look like any child
playing with cats
in the daylight
in Warsaw,
my Jewish armband
burned with the rags I wore
when I escaped from the Ghetto.

I wear my Polish look,
I walk my Polish walk.
Polish words float from my lips
and I am almost safe,
almost invisible,
moving through Krasinski Square
past the dizzy girls riding the merry-go-round.

My brave sister,

Mira,

all that is left of our family,

my brave sister

tells me the plan,

the newest plan

to smuggle food inside the Ghetto.

Her friends will come on the train,

carrying satchels

filled

not with clothes or books,

but bread, oats and sugar.

I know the openings in the Wall.

The cats have taught me.

I show Mira on a map her friend Arik has drawn.

"Every crack will be filled with food," Mira says,

bringing our thin soup to simmer on the ring.

I ask to smuggle the bread

through the spot near Krasinski Square

where Michal lives on the other side of the Wall.

Mira knows the danger,

but she nods.

I fall back on to the mattress

and the big room dances with light.

But on the day,

when the train is already rolling toward Warsaw,

Arik, breathless, bursts into our room

and says the Gestapo

know of the train and the satchels,

and they'll be waiting at the station with their dogs

to sniff out the smugglers.

The look that passes between Arik and Mira

frightens me more

than a knock on the door in the night.

I cannot stay inside.

Instead,

I wear my Polish look,

I walk my Polish walk.

Polish words float from my lips

as I move through Krasinski Square,

singing a nonsense song.

The cats come from the cracks in the Wall,

the dark corners,

the openings in the rubble.

And I know what we must do.

We gather the cats,

one by one,

Mira and Arik, Henryk and Marek,

Hanna and Anna, Tosia and Stasia,

we gather the cats into baskets

CLARE COUNTY LIBRARIES

and head to the station,

where we spread out,

waiting for the train,

behind the Gestapo and their straining,

snarling dogs.

Suddenly steam and the scream of the whistle.

The train pulls in,

passengers stream off.

The dogs are set loose,

their sharp barks echo through the station.

They fly towards

the men and women,

the girls and boys

with the strong scent of bread, oats and sugar about them.

But before the dogs can reach their prey,

we open our
baskets
and let the cats
loose.

The station explodes into chaos
as frenzied dogs turn
their wild hunger on the cats,
who flee in every direction,
slipping through cracks,
into dark corners,
between openings.

The smuggled food

vanishes from the station,

vanishes from our side of Warsaw,

through the Wall, over the Wall, under the Wall,

into the Ghetto.

Including my basket,

with a loaf of bread

for Michal,

taken by grateful hands.

And the music from the merry-go-round

floats in the air, rising, tinsel-bright,

above Krasinski Square.

CLARE COUNTY LIBRARIES

AUTHOR'S NOTE

In 2001, I came across a short article about cats outwitting the Gestapo at the railway station in Warsaw during World War II. I couldn't get the story out of my mind, so I went in search of accounts of the Warsaw Ghetto and the Jewish Resistance in Poland. The two most valuable sources I found were the Ringelblum archives and Adina Blady Szwajger's book, *I Remember Nothing More*. Mira, the fictional older sister of the narrator in *The Cats in Krasinski Square*, was inspired by Adina Blady Szwajger. I owe the texture and substance of this book to Szwajger's account of her experience with the Jewish Resistance.

HISTORICAL NOTE

In late September 1939, at the beginning of World War II, Warsaw, the capital of Poland, fell into the hands of the attacking Germans. The Gestapo (German State Police) forced all Jewish men, women and children from Warsaw and its surrounding towns to live on certain streets within the invaded city. If non-Jews lived in any of the buildings on these streets, they received orders to move out. A high brick wall was built to keep the Jewish people in, separated from the Aryans (non-Jewish "whites") who lived on the other side. By the time the Gestapo had collected all the local Jewish people, the overcrowding inside the Warsaw Ghetto had created conditions ripe for disease and hunger. Every day, hundreds of men, women and children fell in the Ghetto streets, too ill to take another step. And in those streets, they died.

In July 1942, the Germans began carrying out their plan to relocate the Warsaw Jews. The youngest and oldest disappeared from the Ghetto first, at the rate of 2,000, then 10,000, then 20,000 people per day. The weakest were killed before they ever left Warsaw. Eventually the Germans emptied the Ghetto of all Jews except those working in war plants.

Even though they were physically and emotionally exhausted, many Jews fought back. Thousands of brave young men and women planned ways to upset the Nazis' plans. These Jews formed an opposition group, causing trouble for the Germans whenever possible. At great risk, these daring Jews smuggled people out of, and weapons, food and medicine into, the Ghetto, saving thousands of Jewish lives.

In April 1943, the German army had every advantage when the last battle against the Warsaw Ghetto fighters began. And yet this handful of sick, starving and injured civilians held off an army of trained German soldiers for over forty days. As the Germans bombed and set buildings on fire, the Jewish Resistance, leading their attacks from basements, attics and hidden passages, knew the chance for a victory over the Germans was impossible. Yet even after the buildings within the Ghetto were flattened, small pockets of fighters rose up against the Nazis, waging a war until death.

Not every Jew died. Those who passed as Polish on the Aryan side of the Wall aided the escape of several hundred Jewish fighters. These daring warriors struggled out of the Ghetto, neck-deep through the filth and stench of the Warsaw sewers, towards freedom. The last survivors of the Jewish Ghetto came forward at the end of the war to tell the terrible truth of the acts carried out by the Nazis.

In memory of my mother, Fran Levin
K.H.

For my father, Aldren Auld Watson —
my teacher, mentor, colleague, and collaborator
W.W.

CL208771